Giants

Wendy Blaxland
illustrated by Christina Brimage

Blaxland, Wendy, 1949–.
Giants.

ISBN 1 86388 603 6.

1. Readers (Primary). I. Brimage, Christina.
II. Title. (Series: Reading discovery.)

428.6

First published in 1996 by Scholastic Australia Pty Limited ACN 000 614 577,
PO Box 579, Gosford 2250. Also in Sydney, Brisbane, Melbourne, Adelaide and Perth.

Printed in Hong Kong.

9 8 7 6 5 4 3 2 1   6 7 8 9 / 9

SCHOLASTIC
SYDNEY AUCKLAND NEW YORK TORONTO LONDON

Giants in the garden,
tramp, tramp, tramp!

We can hear them coming, stamp, stamp, stamp!

Splashing in the puddles,
running on the grass.

We had better hide
until the giants pass.

Giants, please be careful.
Don't make such a fuss.

Jump in puddles all you like,

but please don't jump on us!